For my publisher and best friend,
Klaus Flugge

Copyright © 2004 by David Mckee

All rights reserved · CIP data available

Published in the United States 2004 by Handprint Books

413 Sixth Avenue, Brooklyn, New York 11215

www.handprintbooks.com

First American Edition

Originally Published in Great Britain by Andersen Press Ltd.

Printed in Singapore

ISBN 1-59354-078-7

2 4 6 8 10 9 7 5 3 1

THE CONQUERORS

David McKee

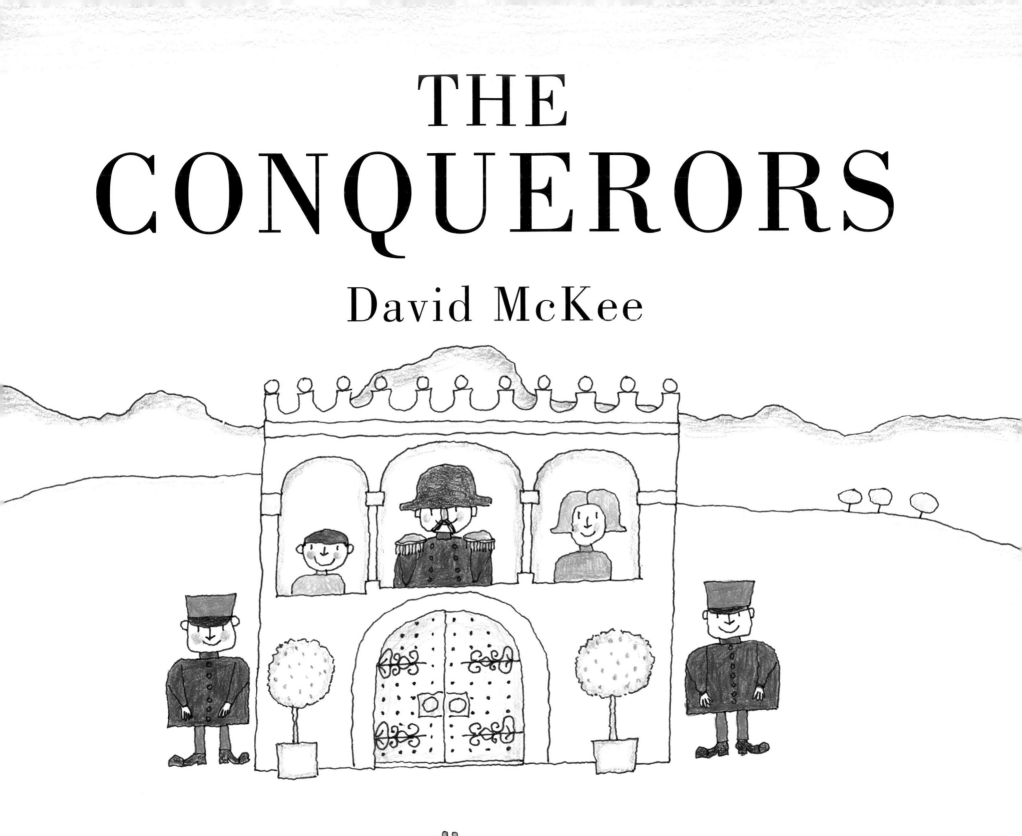

HANDPRINT BOOKS 🖐 BROOKLYN, NEW YORK

There was once a large country that was ruled by a General.
The people believed that their way of life was the best.
They had a very strong army, and they had the cannon.

From time to time the General would take his army and attack a nearby country.
"It's for their own good," he said. "So they can be like us."

The other countries resisted—but, in the end,
they were always conquered.

Eventually the General ruled all the countries except one . . .
This was such a small country that the General had never
bothered to invade it. But now it was the only one left.
So one day the General and his army set out again.

The small country surprised the General.
It had no army and offered no resistance.
Instead, the people greeted the soldiers as if they were welcome guests.
The General installed himself in the most comfortable house
while the soldiers lodged with families.

Each morning the General paraded his soldiers and then wrote letters home
to his wife and son.
The soldiers talked with the people, played their games, listened to their stories,
joined in their songs, and laughed at their jokes.

The food was different from their own.
They watched it being prepared, then ate it. It was delicious.
With nothing else to do, the soldiers helped the people with their work.

When the General realized what was happening, he was furious.
He sent the soldiers home . . .

. . . and replaced them with fresh ones.

But the new soldiers behaved just as the others had. The General realized that he didn't need a large army there. He decided to return home and leave just a few soldiers to occupy the country.

Once the General was gone, those soldiers hung up their uniforms and joined in the daily life.

The General returned home triumphant, with his soldiers
chanting as usual:

"We are the conquerors.
We are the conquerors."

He was glad to be back, although somehow it was different. The cooking smelled of the cooking of the little country. People were playing games from the little country. Even some clothes were those of the little country.
He smiled and thought: "Ah! The spoils of war."

That night, when he put his son to bed,
his son asked him to sing to him.
So he sang the only songs he could remember.
The songs of the little country—
the little country he had conquered.